Amazing Teddy
— and the —
BEATITUDES

Bill Van Dusen

Available from Amazon.com and other online stores
Available on Kindle and online store

Cover design by Erin Ewasko

ISBN: 978-0-9979225-0-9(sc)
ISBN: 978-0-9979225-1-6(e)

Library of Congress Control Number: 2016913023

Printed in the United States of America

Argyll Jack Publisher

I dedicate this book to my uncles, John and Nateli, who sacrificed their lives for all of us in World War II.
I dedicate this book to all Americans who love, honor, protect and preserve the United States of America.

Romans 5:1-5 New Revised Standard Version (NRSV)

Therefore, since we are justified by faith, we have peace with God through our Lord Jesus Christ, through whom we have obtained access to this grace in which we stand; and we boast in our hope of sharing the glory of God. And not only that, but we also boast in our sufferings, knowing that suffering produces endurance, and endurance produces character, and character produces hope, and hope does not disappoint us, because God's love has been poured into our hearts through the Holy Spirit that has been given to us.

Acknowledgements

To Karen Pedersen, Eudcay Jones, Carole Bagin and Sue Genter thank you for your invaluable help in preparation for this book.

To my loving wife, Linda, without your help my life would be miserable and there would be no book. Thanks for keeping me on task.

Thanks to everyone who offered their interest and encouragement.

Thank you St. Bridget of Kildare, St. Anthony of Padua, St. Padre Pio of Pietrelcina, St. Gerard of Majella, St. Joseph and the Blessed Mother for all your help.

A special mention for Jack. Thank you for showing us how to live each day to the fullest.

To Davy and Bo, the real masters of the house, thank you for preventing me from being too serious.

Thanks Mom for everything.

Teddy was bigger than life but he did not know it.

Even as a kitten he could climb higher, run faster and leap anywhere.

He loved to wrestle too.

To scuffle with his brother Rocky was the best part of the day.

The brothers loved each other most of all. However, things changed when Rocky got sick, no more races and wrestling.

Teddy spent long hours watching over Rocky.

He helped Rocky as much as he could. Night vigils over the stricken Rocky exhausted them both until the day that Rocky died.

Teddy was confused and felt lost without Rocky. Teddy said to no one, "My chest hurts."

Big Teddy was lonely without Rocky. He slept too much and ate too much.

Dr. Morgan said, "He is a big boy but almost 21 pounds is a bit too much for him to carry."

The result was a reduction in Teddy's dry food to help him lose some weight. At first Teddy thought Mamma Linda was punishing him, but finally decided Mamma would never do that. Still he slept under the big bed and slept on the couch and even fell asleep at the window watching the birds.

Teddy thought he must do something to feel better. He felt lost and decided to go on a journey to find himself.

He called it, "my walk-about." Teddy Bear first learned of "walk-about" from his mentor and big brother, Casey. Casey learned of this from his older sibling gentle Max. Every day he searched the house for the missing part. He understood that Rocky was gone, but he needed to make peace with this situation.

Finally, honorable Teddy thought that this must be the walk in the desert that he heard about. He said, "To get un-lost I must look inside myself. But how? I remember Rocky said we can pray about things. So I will."

So Teddy followed Rocky's wonderful advice even though he did not understand it. Teddy appealed to God for help. He prayed hard for 100 days.

Teddy prayed, "Jesus, help me." And "Jesus, be my friend."

Teddy learned, "Hey, I feel good when I pray. So I will continue to pray with all my might."

"Hmm… I can't reckon it out for myself," he mused. "Rocky told me to ask God to explain it and then listen for an answer. Yes, I will look for Him everywhere."

One day after his walk-about Teddy stopped in his tracks and felt a warmth all over his body. The Holy Spirit ignited Teddy's heart with joy and he purred loud and strong.

Teddy purred non-stop for the rest of his life. Like a medieval monk he turned each and every action into some kind of prayer.

Big Teddy learned that God answers our prayers in His time and not our time.

Teddy praised God for the rest of his days. Big Teddy continued to pray and things felt better and he got better.

He prayed, "Lord Jesus Christ, Son of the living God, have mercy on us all. We praise you every day. Please, God, bless, heal and protect us. Amen."

One day Mamma Linda said, "Our Teddy needs some brothers to play with. We will help him with two new wonderful buddies."

Solitary Teddy lived 148 days without Rocky. He did the best he could. Wrestling with Papa Bill was fun but not like sparring with Rocky.

Then on April 9, 2011 it happened. Mamma's big surprise!

Teddy did not see it coming!

Being the biggest and strongest and fastest was meaningless without his brother. All this was trivial now. He felt hollow inside. Hollow and lost. But this? But this was almost more than he could handle.

Mamma shattered Teddy's deep thoughts, "Look, Teddy Bear, we got you baby brothers!"

Teddy was stunned. There they were … two kittens. They looked nothing like Rocky. So how could they be his baby brothers?

Next Mamma did an awful thing. She opened the pet carrier and the two creatures charged Teddy. Teddy froze in his tracks as the boys rubbed on him and sniffed him and played with his tail.

Teddy thought, "What am I to do?"

Mamma answered with great joy, "Teddy, you have brothers to love."

Teddy Bear answered, "Say what?!"

Mamma continued, "The tall one is Jack and the tiny one is Davy."

All Teddy could do was stand still with his mouth open as the boys continued to rub and smell again and again.

Wow! Brothers to love!

The kittens ran everywhere. Teddy tried to look at them carefully as they darted in every direction.

Amazing Teddy noticed they had big eyes and big ears. And gangly legs and big feet. And no manners.

Then Teddy noticed they were both tabby and white. Tabby and white!

"They look like me!"

"Well, maybe I can teach them something. Manners would be a good place to start," reflected Teddy.

At that instant jaunty Jack and dandy Davy leaped upon Teddy and they fell into a pile. The kittens laughing loudly and with Teddy trying to be "two good boys." (This was an expression that Mamma Linda used when Rocky and Teddy were little.) The mayhem persisted until bed time.

"What was Mamma thinking? I do miss Rocky so much it hurts but now these kittens are driving me crazy. I feel lost and confused. What's to do? If Rocky was here he would tell me what to do. I need to discern (figger in Cat) what it all means. Rocky always said to talk to God. That's what I can do. I will ask God for an answer. So I will."

And Teddy prayed. Teddy prayed as much as the kittens allowed. Three days later Teddy awoke from a brief nap relieved. He remembered that Rocky once said we can pray always about things.

"He was right! Maybe I can deal with those two little ruffians and help Mamma too."

"To get un-lost I must look inside my heart and talk to God some more. I will pray my best for Jesus to relieve my pains and confusion."

So he prayed again. "Jesus, be my friend. Help me, Jesus."

And Teddy prayed harder than ever. Big Teddy asked God for help every day for another 100 days.

He observed, "I feel good when I pray. I will pray every day."

During these days the Holy Spirit changed Teddy. His heart felt thrilled and he purred loud and strong. Silent no more he talked and purred and chirped and smiled more.

Indeed, Teddy found his voice.

Jack and Davy were still little wild men but Teddy Bear felt better about the boys being here.

Teddy tried to show the kittens what Rocky taught him. He thought with powerful purpose to recall his brother's words. He saw Mamma's Bible and rightly guessed the book contained all the answers.

"But I can't read. I need some help now."

Little by little some of it came back to him.

"Honor thy father and mother. Have mercy…be merciful. Do not steal." (Cat Logic: Now this is hard for cats. All cats know food tastes better when it is stolen. But he tried his best.)

"Like Papa Bill says, 'We are moving closer to heaven one day at a time, even if it is only a quarter of an inch forward at a time.'"

BEATITUDES

Then one quiet night a gentle breeze roused Teddy and it happened—Malcolm arrived.

Big Teddy was watching over the sleeping brothers. Even though they had their own beds, they loved to sleep together in a pile.

Bear would use this time to catnap and muse on the events of the day. It was at these times Teddy's sharp ears would hear sounds but did not recognize them.

Often he would see a shimmering of light briefly across the room only to watch it dance and quickly vanish.

Tonight Malcolm, Mamma's guardian angel, vividly stood by the kitchen table and smiled at Teddy.

Teddy thought, "My imagination is flowing."
He shook his head.
"I'm a fuzzy-duddy."

At times like this he would make a mental list of scary things in his life or things that he loved. This was a comfort to him.

Such as:

1. He learned to work his mouth as if eating or drinking when he wanted food from his family.

2. He laughed when he remembered Gramma Florence taught him about "mangia, mangia" at suppertime. He smiled, "I can eat in two languages."

3. And he was happy he had learned to say "muh-muh." It made him feel good that he could call to Mamma Linda whenever he wanted.

*** *** *** *** ***

But this time his visitor was real. The guardian angel, Malcolm, was sent from God to help Teddy.

The angel said, "Be not afraid. Teddy, I have words for you…. God wants you to embrace His Word."

"Blessed are the poor in spirit, for theirs is the kingdom of heaven."

Teddy quickly looked at the boys. They slept soundly.

He blinked hard several times and hushed, "What's that?"

Malcolm replied, "This means to be humble. We should put others first and place all our cares in God. God should be first in everything. After Him comes your baby brothers."

Teddy thought that even though Jack and Davy tormented him he would try his best to watch over and protect the boys like a good shepherd.

Yes. Teddy could learn to do many things.

Teddy tried to be their sheep dog. He chose to guard and protect his brothers faithfully.

Calling them brothers made him feel good inside.

Again Malcolm spoke,
"Blessed are those who mourn, for they will be comforted."

Teddy lowered his head and shook and shuddered quietly.

Malcolm said nothing and placed his large right hand on Teddy's head. The angel shimmered from time to time. After resting there he gently stroked Teddy's big head and the big cat became calm.

Teddy hung his head and his body quivered in a great sigh of grief.

Malcolm said, "I know."

After a pause, Teddy realized that Malcolm knew how much he missed Rocky.

"Teddy, remember God is our Father."

Teddy squinted and replied, "Rocky used to say that all the time."

Malcolm declared,
"Blessed are the meek, for they will inherit the earth."

"The meek horse wins the race, Teddy. This does not mean weakness. It is a special kind of self-control. And it is a power that keeps you under control in the face of death and danger. It is the power that fights off anger and dissolves discouragement and 'inherit the earth' hints at something new coming to you."

Radiant Malcolm smiled, "Someday you will become a little Moses."

Teddy stared at the angel and asked, "What's meek?"

Malcolm said, "I'll explain it this way. In the South, horse trainers say 'the meekest horse wins the race.' This means you follow directions. You replace attitude with your coaches' teachings or better still God the Father."

Quickly Malcolm pronounced,
"Blessed are those who hunger and thirst for righteousness, for they will be filled."

"This means we try to always be at our best. Do it right and never shirk your duty. Also, try to make others around you even better too. Be a real team player. OK?"

"I think so…" (Teddy blinked and looked up at Malcolm with wide eyes.)

"You long to be good…don't you?"

Precious Teddy purred and "chirped" softly.

"Make your last action as good as the first," advised Malcolm.

"Teddy,
Blessed are the merciful, for they will receive mercy."

Malcolm said, "If you reach out to others and forgive them, your patience and love and understanding will be repaid with mercy. This tells us to forgive others. Being merciful helps the world thrive. Mercy eventually chases misery down. Many of the great saints were filled with mercy. Wrap others in a cloak of compassion, like St. Francis of Assisi, St. Gerard of Majella and St. Anthony of Padua."

Teddy whispered, "St. Mother Teresa and St. Padre Pio, too?"

"Yes," smiled Malcolm in a soft glow of golden light.

Malcolm uttered, "Naturally these saints can direct us to the next Beatitude."

"Our Lord and Savior taught us…
Blessed are the pure in heart, for they will see God."

"Ask God how can I help others? How can I do good?"

Teddy asked, "Can I make God smile?"

Malcolm laughed, "Close enough, Big Fella."

Malcolm intoned, "Jesus wants us to think about what we think about. Seeing God in heaven depends upon having the right kind of heart, Teddy, pure in heart means to be clean of heart. It means all evil is driven away. Pure in heart means you will see God as I do."

Malcolm said, "Remember when your Cat-Mamma said, 'Be two good boys'?"

Teddy, "Uh-huh."

"That is about the next Beatitude and the importance of peace," said Malcolm. "Purity of heart helps direct you to a place of peace. It is the fragrance of your heart."

"Blessed are the peacemakers, for they will be called children of God."

"God wants us to pursue peace and keep the peace. He wants us to live in such a way that others will be drawn to us. We are to illuminate the Gospel (God's Way) for all to see. Be attractive of heart."

Malcolm said, "Peacemakers recognize the wrong and try to fix it. Even if it costs you your own peace and requires suffering. God wants us to help the helpless and defend the defenseless."

Teddy asked, "How about, 'Peace be with you'?"

Malcolm said, "Yes. Indeed. That's a start, a good start."

Teddy's eyes fluttered, "And three good boys."

Malcolm smiled, "Now Teddy, the next one is a tough one, but it is essential."

"Blessed are those who are persecuted for righteousness' sake, for theirs is the kingdom of heaven."

Teddy Bear looked perplexed.

Malcolm explained, "You know, Teddy, it is unfortunate, not everyone likes cats. You will encounter rancor and hatred just because of who you are. Especially for all your goodness. Jesus endured hostility and persecution but, stay committed to God's way and you will be rewarded by our heavenly Father."

And Malcolm quickly continued:
"Blessed are you when they insult you and persecute you and utter every kind of evil against you {falsely} because of me."

Then Malcolm sang powerfully, "Rejoice and be glad, for your reward will be great in heaven for in the same way they persecuted the prophets who were before you. Amen."

"Purr, Teddy. Purr for everyone you meet," he said. "Purr all the time. Always. And let your light shine for all to see. Especially the little ones."

"Remember, Teddy, Jesus gave us these words to help us be strong and peaceful. We know them as the 'Beatitudes' today."

Malcolm began to turn away but paused and said to Big Teddy, "And yes, you will be with Rocky again. In heaven."

Malcolm stood in the warm golden light.

Then the angel departed. Teddy blinked and stared at the spot where Malcolm had stood.

Teddy thought, "Jesus is my friend. He makes me confident and unafraid. Now I can help Mamma and the boys. Bye, Malcolm—where did he go?"

Teddy blinked and looked for Malcolm but he had vanished.

Big Teddy put his head on his paws and thought. He was still thinking about what Malcolm had said when the sun rose.

CAT TALES

As time passed things got better and his heartaches healed. Smiles and joy returned for Teddy. Play was the rule of the day. Teddy, the gentle and graceful lion, cared for his mamma's boys.

Big Teddy rightly chose to work on Jack and Davy's manners. And things got better. Of course the kittens still continued their wild man ways.

Teddy remembered Gramma Florence saying, "You are good boys when you sleep."

Laughing Teddy thought, "Truer words were never spoken." He smiled and wondered on his purpose.

Teddy sat up all night and kept watch over his brothers, "Goodnight, boys."

*** *** *** *** ***

From time to time Teddy still thought about little Rocky and how much he ached when he thought of his dear brother. Rocky was an innocent boy so why was he snatched from us?

The big cat thought and thought but without success. "I'll continue to talk to God and ask Him for meaning."

Teddy prayed, "God help me when I get gloomy."

When there were quiet times, Teddy chose to tell the boys stories.

And he knew best the hero tales of his brother Rocky.

The kittens would sometimes ask Teddy to tell his own stories.

This would make Teddy become shy and say, "Aw, you don't want to hear about me. Now Rocky, he was something else!"

So Teddy regaled the boys about how Rocky was fast and strong and fearless. After Rocky got sick he took to watching TV with the family. He loved all the music shows and adventure movies. But he loved sports in season, especially baseball.

Surprisingly Jack and Davy were interested in Rocky's love of baseball.

Jack asked, "What's that?"

Davy echoed, "Yeah, what's baseball?"

As best as he could, Teddy related Rocky's love for baseball. Rocky would sit in his little red bed and root for all the players. He would know the count and the score and tell everybody the number of outs. He cheered for every player. Even the umpires.

Rocky liked one player the best.

He would announce at the start of some games, "I am 'Little Chooch.' I try my best, I help my teammates. I love my team. I want to be brave and strong and smart and fearless just like my favorite catcher. I am a leader. Play ball!"

Telling this story warmed Teddy's heart. Jack and Davy loved the tales of Rocky and baseball, too.

Teddy thought often life makes no sense. Baseball has rules and makes sense. The events inside the white lines make sense. Rocky was good but he died so young.

Ted thought his brother was not "out" and he was not guilty of anything. Sometimes he shook with anger when he dwelt on this.

Teddy said out loud, "My brother was not guilty!"

Then he heard a silent voice inside whisper, "Jesus was a guiltless man, too."

This gave Teddy a new reason to ponder and it settled him.

But most of all they lived and died with the events of the home team.

Jack loved the big hits and the big hitters, especially walk off homers that disappeared into the night sky.

The boys laughed when the pitcher had to play left field and cheered when he caught the first out of the inning.

Davy loved the squirrel that ran across home plate during a big game.

Jack and Davy would get so excited.

Both would race to the TV and try to catch the ball.

Teddy reminded Jack to take it easy. The guardian cat worried about Jack's bad heart.

Kind Teddy Bear helped the two boys grow up. His gentle sacrifice was not readily evident but was essential.

The boys would ask, "Big Bear, tell us about Rocky. Or, what about Gramma stories?"

Teddy mused, "Stories. God loves stories. God tells us wonderful stories. All His tales are amazing. So beautiful that even angels stop to listen."

And so T-Bear spoke slowly, "Gramma loved baseball. She and Rocky would watch all the games on TV, day and night. But Gramma did not like today's players as much. She said they lacked purpose. They went through the motions. Rocky agreed even though his favorite player was an exception. The catcher was wise and strong and smart and brave. He was the hardest worker too. Gramma agreed."

And that end came suddenly when one of their heroes struck out to make the last out of the first round playoffs. He came crashing to the ground with an injury. He fell like a redwood tree.

Davy said, "He tried his best."

Jack said, "He is a giant—just like you, Teddy."

All three cats sighed together.

Teddy said, "Let's all say a prayer for our big first baseman. He hurt his ankle real bad. He is gonna need lots of medicine and lots of prayers."

The boys had no way of knowing how badly their hero was hurt.

Jack whispered, "Rise again."

The three Maine Coons bowed their heads.

Teddy spoke, "Heavenly Father, please bless, heal and protect our team, especially our big first baseman, and all other ball players in battle out there. And please heal these two boys. God bless my brothers. Amen."

Teddy pronounced, "Just wait till next year. They won't beat us."

The boys chimed, "Yeah!"

Teddy identified with the big slugger. He thought of his own aches and pains and prayed for the big fella. He thought maybe the Beatitudes that Malcolm brought that night would help here.

Teddy mused that when you are big and strong nobody notices your aches and heartaches.

Yes…the Beatitudes will help here.

HEROES

Later Teddy taught Jack and Davy there were things more important than games. Stories like the sacrifices of Gramma's brothers help us live our lives. Uncle John and Uncle Nateli went off to war to protect their loved ones. They were heroes. Gramma Florence called her brothers "eroi."

You have to be in combat to know and understand it. Sometimes we can only learn what is important through the heroic actions of others. But the Beatitudes shed light on the loss of the Uncles.

The Beatitudes were especially a help and comfort for Teddy.

For the next few weeks Teddy purred and purred. He felt better and noticed the world seemed better too. It had the aroma of roses. This made him think of the Blessed Mother.

The only thing that perplexed him was Malcolm's final words.

"And yes, you will be with Rocky again. In heaven."

Saturday night was movie night. Even though Teddy did not like popcorn, he enjoyed comedy films. He laughed at Jack and Davy playing "ball" with the popcorn until they fell asleep.

Teddy reveled in being with his darling brothers now. He loved them both with all his might.

However, he carried a fear for Jack. A fear that he might reach too far one day.

Teddy's sides hurt from laughing at his little brothers and Robin Williams in the movie. Then Teddy realized just as Robin Williams brought laughter and blessings to people, he could bring joy for others, too.

Teddy went to sleep that night smiling in his heart and happy that he found a clue to his puzzle.

"Purr, purr, purr."

One day Davy asked again, "Big Bear, tell us more Gramma stories."

"Well, I will if I can. Gramma Florence told them to Rocky mostly. But I'll try."

"Yeah," gasped Jack.

"Who are the faces on the wall in Gramma's room?"

Teddy mused, "Good question. Those two men are great heroes."

Jack's ears perked up. "They are Gramma Florence's two brothers who were killed in World War II."

Both boys chimed, "What's that?"

"Well, sometimes the world gets in a fight that can't be stopped easily."

"What about a 'time-out'?" Davy asked.

"No, sometimes there are men so bad that no time-out will ever work. They kill other people for fun and for power."

Davy and Jack were shocked. They mouthed, "Gosh."

And so Teddy, the big bear-cat, began the story as he knew it.

*** *** *** *** ***

Gramma Florence came from a family of twelve children. Eight boys and four girls. Most of them were born in Sicily, but she was born in America.

John and Nateli were her youngest brothers. Mostly the young trio of kids spent time together. They lived on a farm at first but later the family moved to the city.

The farm years were the best. It was hard work on the farm but they loved playing games, fishing and picking grapes. Their father made his own wine. Their mother was a great cook. Her homemade prosciutto was the best. They grew tomatoes, beans and peaches. Pigs and cows were raised on the farm, too.

One day wicked men conspired to spread their darkness all over the world. They threatened the weak and attacked the strong trying to crush the world into their mad image.

"They were bullies?" Davy said incredulously.

"Indeed."

Uncle John and Uncle Nateli joined the army to fight for the USA.

Gramma Florence spoke of her brothers' letters from the battlefields of North Africa, Sicily, Italy and France. She was very scared about their safety and cherished the letters over the years.

*** *** *** *** ***

Uncle Nateli was thrilled by wildlife. He marveled at flying fish he saw while on board the ship to Europe. He was disappointed that he never saw any whales. Nateli's love of animals was rivaled only by his sense of humor. He kept everyone entertained with his comments and observations.

Nateli seemed to revel in his parents' homeland of Sicily. He loved the sun and the food, especially pasta, wine, grapes, olives and lemons. He was amazed that he could pick lemons from trees there.

The climate was hot and dry but he loved it. He loved even the donkeys that he saw everywhere.

Uncle John was gentle and quiet. He was very resourceful. John cared so very much for others. He showed his caring by catching fish from the stream and cooking for the other men. He found ways to buy butter and eggs from the farmers.

Even though he was a Staff Sargent, he was not too important to roll up his sleeves and get dirty. He cooked for his men, and it was tasty. Once he even milked a cow. He laughed when the cow tried to kick him. "She didn't know I was an old hand at it."

John was involved in many conflicts with the enemy. The medals he earned proved how he faced death head on protecting his men in battle. The army said it best:

> "When a strong enemy patrol approached his platoon's position, Sergeant Visalli unhesitatingly advanced and engaged the foe. Although outnumbered and subjected to heavy fire, he continued to press forward until he destroyed the entire hostile group."

Most of all John shared his courage. He would try to give hope to everyone no matter how dark it seemed. And he asked about everyone in his letters.

Both boys were grateful to speak Italian with the people. It was a great comfort for them.

They were proud to see Sicilian men making wine "just like Pop did."

John met a group of Italian POWs and found one who was from his father's ancestral province in Sicily. The man said he even knew of other Visalli relatives.

John always ended his letters beautifully.

> If you don't hear from me in a little while,
> don't worry about it. As there isn't anything
> to worry about. Closing for now.
>   Love,
>   John

This story of John and Nateli had a curious power over Teddy. It spoke to him in whispers and winds at all hours of the day and night.

*** *** *** *** ***

Then late one night Teddy was awakened to the sound of great wings. He looked around for birds but there were none.

He thought he heard distant singing. Singing and wings.

Teddy quickly arose and strode with strength into the kitchen. He stiffened and assumed a mighty warrior stance.

Teddy cried out, "Who's there? What's that?"

Stillness fell around him and he heard one voice breathe, "Remember the Beatitudes. Remember how to live."

And then it stopped.

He checked on the boys and they lay sound asleep. Teddy realized that must have been just for him.

"What am I to do with it?"

Since that night snippets of the Beatitudes played in Teddy's head and heart.

In a sports sense he was relegated to playing defense. That is protecting his little brothers became his life's work now. Honoring his mamma and papa was paramount too.

He thought, "I want to be like Nateli and John."

He became "Good Boy Teddy" and "T-Bear" and "Brother." Also "Ted." He answered to these names with great waves of purrs and chirps. Teddy was dreaming of being a giant maned lion in Africa watching his cubs when Jack nudged him from his reverie with a question.

Jack said, "Hey – Hey – Hey- Big guy, what's a name? Your name is Teddy and my name is Jack and he is Davy… but what's it all mean?"

Teddy smiled and sighed, "Well, Clever One, your name is Jack. It is an old name, with confusing origins, meaning 'God is gracious.' Some say it means 'truthful.' But this is you. I think that is you because you are so quiet and direct. You speak from the heart. Really, you do everything from the heart."

"Wow…" mused Jack.

Davy was impatient, "Me, me, me next."

Teddy smiled, "I have learned about names from Mamma. I learn by staying still and listening with my best ears. Davy means 'Beloved One.' Love leaps from God and He wants you to bring love to all others."

"Love? No 'rassling'?

"You can wrestle, but no 'hinny biting'."

They all laughed.

"Davy, you should close your mouth and open your ears and eyes and think about what is said. That's just for you. You should always try to live up to your name because it is a gift and a blessing."

Ted offered, "And my name means, 'Gift of God.' I think it means that God wants me to help Him in this world. You know like I watch over you two guys. Work and prayer are connected."

Davy sighed, "Big Bear, today was a good day."

"Yeah," echoed Jack.

*** *** *** *** ***

Teddy taught the boys many things. There were more important things than games. Sometimes Teddy spoke of knowledge of cat lore. But more often he sang stories and poems for their enjoyment.

He loved telling them of the beauty of his brother Rocky. Yes, Rocky was full of gentleness and fiery strength and love.

Teddy wondered why death wanted Rocky so soon. Perhaps Jesus could explain it. Teddy vowed to ask Him.

LIVING THE BEATITUDES

One night as they talked about the love and strength of brothers the kittens interrupted Ted's story.

"Tell us more about Gramma's brothers!"

"Yeah...tell us."

Together they uttered, "Tell us about Uncle John and Uncle Nateli that went off to war."

Teddy blinked at their abruptness. Then he pronounced, "Good idea."

"Were they afraid?" asked Jack.

Like a bolt of fire from the night sky it became clear to Teddy that the mystery of the uncles burned white hot. Like phosphorus.

Bear comforted the kittens, "Of course they were. But faith in God helped them endure the bad times. Boys, I now see how all this is connected to our lives. Gramma's brothers lived the Beatitudes."

Their story goes like this:
"Honor thy father and mother: John and Nateli went to war because they loved their mom and dad."

"Have mercy…be merciful: John saved the lives of many of his men in combat. Nateli helped his mates as much as he could. Both respected the feelings of their family and friends in their letters home. And they loved their country, too."

"Do not steal: They paid the farmers for all the eggs and butter and other food they bought. They did not steal." (Big Bear thought the boys needed to know this.)

Teddy continued, "Blessed are the poor in Spirit, for theirs is the Kingdom of Heaven: Boys, both uncles were humble. They put others first and trusted in God. Amen."

"Blessed are those who mourn, for they will be comforted: Yes, John and Nateli grieved for the loss of their buddies killed in battle."

"They lost their buddies? That's sad," Jack whispered with a tear.

Davy hung his head.

Teddy reminded them, "Boys, remember God is our Father."

"Blessed are the meek, for they will inherit the earth: This does not mean weakness. It is a special kind of power and control that dissolves discouragement and fights fear. As good soldiers, they followed orders. John and Nateli had great big hearts and they were full of love."

"Blessed are those who hunger and thirst for righteousness, for they will be filled: This means we always give our best. Always do right and help others do right."

"Blessed are the merciful, for they will receive mercy: John and Nateli carried no anger in their hearts. Just love. They knew how to forgive."

Jack asked, "Were they like saints?"

Davy echoed, "Were they?"

Teddy answered, "I suppose you could call them that. They would probably disagree. But I think so."

"Blessed are the pure in heart, for they will see God: This is a hard one but it is a club anyone can enter. It is your choice. This means to have a clean heart. A heart with all evil chased away. OK?"

"OK, ok," echoed the little boys.

"Blessed are the peacemakers, for they will be called children of God: God wants us to seek peace and keep the peace. To live in a way that will drive out fighting. Peacemakers recognize the wrong and try to fix it. That's what John and Nateli were compelled to do for all of us. It might require suffering. It might even cost you your life. God wants us to help the helpless and defend the defenseless."

Jack, "What?"

Teddy said, "Jack, God said you should live your life as if you would die."

Davy asks, "Always do good? And play hard?"

Teddy answered, "Yes."

"Man, that's hard."

"Yes, Davy, it is, but we can do it."

Jack stared at the floor and said nothing.

"Blessed are those who are persecuted for righteousness sake, for theirs is the Kingdom of Heaven: boys, this means that life can be unfair. No matter how bad it gets, we must still love God. God will be on your side."

"Things can get pretty tough," offered Jack.

"And rough," spoke Davy.

Teddy said, "But if you put on the armor of God you can handle it. Just as Malcolm told me, I will say to you, 'Jesus gave us these words to help make us stronger and peaceful.' These words are for you, too."

The kittens were quiet.

Jack piped up, "So these words are a plan that God wants us to follow."

Davy said, "Yeah, and be brave like Uncle John and Uncle Nateli."

"Indeed," promised Teddy, "and Rocky also."

Teddy purred to himself.

Teddy reminded Jack and Davy it was well after their bedtime.

Teddy looked down on them and said, "Peace be with you."

"And also with you!" yelled Jack and Davy.

And then they scampered off to their little beds.

Teddy spoke aloud, "Yes…Let their names not be forsaken by the minds of men. John and Nateli sacrificed their lives for their loved ones. All of the men did. And much more. Dear Lord, Christ Jesus, have mercy on us. Please bless, heal and protect all of us here in this house. Amen."

The giant cat stood like a Centurion at his post until the walls of the house were roseate and full of the promise of the morning.

Afterward

Teddy died of an undiagnosed condition of HCM (Hypertrophic Cardiomyopathy) on March 11, 2013. He is reunited with his dear brother Rocky in heaven. Teddy spends his days helping St. Michael the Archangel in God's Heavenly Stables. His nights are spent with his brother Rocky in the warm and fragrant glow of Mary's kitchen.

Jack passed away at age 3 on January 13, 2014. He lived an active and full life right to the very end. His severe HCM took him on a sunny afternoon. Thank you God for giving us our Jack. We will always remember "Jack-Jack-Jack."

Gramma Florence joined her Nateli and John and the rest of the family on August 2, 2013.

Nateli   Florence   John

John Visalli

Citation For Bronze Star Medal

John Visalli, 13008933, Staff Sergeant (then corporal), Company C, 16th Infantry.

For heroic achievement in connection with military operations against the enemy in the vicinity of Oran, Algeria, 9 November 1942. When a strong enemy patrol approached his platoon's position, Sergeant Visalli unhesitatingly advanced and engaged the foe. Although outnumbered and subjected to heavy fire, he continued to press forward until he destroyed the entire hostile group. Sergeant Visalli's inspiring heroism reflects great credit on the Service. Residence at enlistment: Woodbury, N.J.

G.O. No. 75
Hq.   1st. U.S. Inf. Div.
5 September 1944

in reply refer to 258,468
Army Service Forces
Kansas City Quartermaster Dept.
Army Effects Bureau
601 Hardesty Avenue
Kansas City, Missouri

Citation For Oak Leaf Cluster to Bronze Star Medal – Posthumous

John Visalli, 13008933, Staff Sergeant, Company C, 16th Infantry.

For heroic achievement in connection with military operations against the enemy in the vicinity of Les Haies, Normandy, France, 2 July 1944. Crossing open terrain under heavy machine gun and small arms fire, Sergeant Visalli administered first aid and assisted in evacuating several critically wounded soldiers. Sergeant Visalli's unselfish heroism is in keeping with the finest tradition of the service.

Residence at enlistment: Woodbury, New Jersey.
Next of kin: Mr. Joseph Visalli, father, 112 West St. Woodbury, New Jersey.

G.O. No. 135
Hq. 1st U.S. Inf. Div.
2 December 1944

Nateli Visalli

Matthew 11:28-30 (NRSV)

Come to me, all you that are weary and are carrying heavy burdens, and I will give you rest. Take my yoke upon you, and learn from me; for I am gentle and humble in heart, and you will find rest for your souls. For my yoke is easy, and my burden is light.